NOV 8 2013
T H E H
D0404141
Neptune

SADDLEBACK™
EDUCATIONAL PUBLISHING

S

THE HEIGHTS™

Blizzard
Camp
Crash
Dive
Neptune
River
Sail
Score
Swamp
Twister

Original text by Ed Hansen
Adapted by Mary Kate Doman

ISBN-13: 978-1-61651-285-9
ISBN-10: 1-61651-285-7
eBook: 978-1-60291-699-9

Printed in Guangzhou, China
0811/CA21101347

16 15 14 13 12 2 3 4 5 6

Chapter 1

It was Saturday. Franco woke up. He smelled bacon. His dad was cooking. Rafael liked to cook. He cooked every weekend. The Silvas were having a family breakfast. They all ate breakfast together.

Franco looked at the clock. It was eight o'clock. He got dressed. Then he went downstairs. His brother and sister were in the kitchen. They were laughing.

"Morning, Franco," said Rafael.

"Hey Dad! What's going on?" Franco asked.

"Dad has a surprise," said Antonio. "We're going fishing. Dad's taking us to Alaska."

"Wow! That's great!" said Franco. "Are all of us going?"

"Nope," Lilia said. "I hate fishing. Mom and I are going to *Tía* Julia's house. We're going to make *pan dulce*. *Abuela* is going to Skype. She's still in Mexico. Then we're going to shop. I would rather shop than fish! You can bring me back some salmon though."

"Don't worry, Lilia," Antonio said. "I'll catch you a ton of salmon! Save me some *pan dulce*. Yum!"

"We'll fly to Alaska. We'll meet my friend Andre Williams. He lives there," Rafael said. "He has a big fishing boat."

"Cool. I'm glad we're going with a pro," said Franco.

Rafael put the bacon on a plate. Then he put pancakes on the table.

"Okay, guys, dig in!" Rafael said.

"Don't forget the syrup," shouted Antonio.

"Or the butter," Lilia said.

Rafael smiled. He handed Antonio the syrup. He passed the butter to Lilia.

Ana Silva walked in the room.

"Thanks for cooking. It smells great," said Ana.

"Here. Have some pancakes," Lilia offered.

"Mom, you guys should come fishing! Alaska is great! Come with us!" cried Antonio.

"Lilia and I want to shop with *Tía* Julia. Your *abuela* is teaching Lilia how to make *pan dulce*. Plus, I love the Heights," said Ana. "I'll leave the adventures to you, Antonio." She smiled.

Chapter 2

Rafael, Franco, and Antonio left two days later. They flew to Juneau.

"Rafael! Rafael!" a voice yelled. It was Andre Williams. He was in baggage claim.

"Welcome to Alaska!" said Andre. "I don't have many guests. Alaska is far," Andre said.

"Hi Andre," Rafael said. "These are my sons, Franco and Antonio."

"Nice to meet you," said Franco.

"Hello, Mr. Williams," Antonio said.

Andre looked at the boys. He smiled.

"Mr. Williams! Who's he? I am Andre. Don't call me Mr. Williams," Andre said. "Or I'll throw you in the ocean!"

Everyone laughed.

"Sure thing, Andre," Franco said. "That water is cold!"

"Yeah, it's freezing," Andre agreed. "You don't want to fall in. Okay. Let's get your bags. We have to get to the boat."

"Sounds good," said Rafael.

They got their bags. Then they headed to the docks. Andre stopped the car. He stopped before getting to the docks. They were at the Mendenhall Glacier. Andre wanted the Silvas to see it.

"Hey! I read about Mendenhall Glacier," Franco said. "It's the most visited glacier in the world."

"You're right, Franco," said Andre. "It's close to Juneau. So a lot of tourists come. The ice is over 200-feet thick!"

"Wow!" Antonio yelled. "That's a ton of ice!"

"Yeah, it is," said Andre. "The glacier is moving. It's getting closer to the ocean. It's melting as it moves. Someday it will be gone!"

"That's crazy," Antonio said. "It's just going to disappear one day?"

"It's not going to disappear. Not for a long time. It will take over 100 years," said Andre.

Andre looked at Rafael.

"The boat is stocked for six days. Is that good? Or should I stop to get more food?" asked Andre.

"No. Six days is fine," said Rafael. "We have to go home next week. Franco has football practice."

"Do you think we'll catch any fish?" asked Antonio.

"Oh, we will," Andre said with a grin.

"Cool! I want to catch a halibut. What are my chances?" Antonio asked.

Andre smiled. "You will catch halibut," he said. "But you may not catch a shooter."

Antonio and Franco looked at each other. They looked puzzled.

"A shooter? I've never heard of it," Franco said. "What kind of fish is a shooter?"

"A shooter is a halibut," replied Andre. "But it weighs over 100 pounds. They are hard to catch. It's too strong. You have to shoot it first. That way it can't get away."

Antonio and Franco were listening. They both wanted to catch a shooter. They couldn't wait to fish.

Chapter 3

Soon they were at the docks. Andre led them to the boat. It was called the *Neptune*.

"There she is," said Andre. "Our home for the next six days."

The *Neptune* was 32-feet. She held a lot of gas. She could travel over 600 miles. That was on one tank! Six days at sea would be no problem.

Andre showed the boys a cabin in the back. It had bunk beds. Andre and Rafael slept in another cabin.

There was also a kitchen. The kitchen had a refrigerator. And it had a stove and sink.

In the center of the deck was the control room. The controls for the ship were there.

They all unpacked. Then they went out. It was their only night to see Juneau. They got back late. The sun was just setting! But it didn't matter. Everyone was tired. They all went to sleep. Tomorrow would be a big day!

They woke up early. Everyone was ready to go. It was exciting! Andre started the boat. The *Neptune* left the dock. They were on their way! They were headed out to sea!

Antonio and Franco stood on the deck. They looked around. They could see mountains. The mountains were covered in snow. It was beautiful.

"How long 'til we can fish?" Franco asked.

"About three hours," said Andre. "We're going around this island. Then we're in the deep sea."

"Cool," said Franco. "Can't wait!"

Rafael cooked breakfast. Everyone ate on the deck. It was a great day already!

The *Neptune* was not fast. She was going about 25 mph. She was a good fishing boat. But she was slow.

Soon, they reached the deep sea. Andre stopped the *Neptune*.

"Grab a rod," said Andre. "It's fishing time! We are fishing for salmon today. There should be a lot here."

Everyone grabbed a rod. They also got bait. They brought the supplies to the deck.

The sun was out. It was 56 degrees. The Silvas felt lucky. This was already a great trip.

They were finally ready to fish. Franco threw his line in the water. Antonio threw his in too.

"Perfect, guys," Rafael said. "Now we wait. The salmon need to bite the bait."

It wasn't hard. Antonio and

Franco were excited. They fished before. But never in Alaska!

Andre watched them.

"Let me know when you get a bite. I'll turn the engine off," Andre said.

Franco and Antonio watched their rods. They waited for the first bite.

The fish weren't biting. Franco and Antonio fished for an hour. They didn't catch anything. Then Franco's rod moved. He pulled. It was heavy.

Chapter 4

"Hey! We've a got a fish," Franco yelled.

Andre heard him. He cut the engine. Rafael ran over to Franco. Andre followed.

Franco pulled on the line. He pulled hard. The salmon fought back. Franco pulled it close to the boat. The fish fought back. It put up a big fight! But it was tired. Franco pulled hard. He pulled the fish closer. Andre grabbed a net. He scooped up the salmon. Franco caught his first salmon!

They all looked at the fish. They weighed it. It was 30 pounds.

"Good job!" Rafael said.

"Yeah," said Antonio. "Lucky catch! That's a big salmon. I bet I'll catch a bigger one."

"You're on," Franco said.

They put the lines back in the water. It was a good day. They caught five more salmon. Antonio won the bet. He caught the biggest salmon. It was 45 pounds.

At the end of the day, Andre cleaned the fish. He showed Franco how to gut the salmon. Then he put them on ice.

"We have over 140 pounds of salmon. Not a bad day's work. Not bad at all!" said Andre.

"Work? Fishing isn't work. Fishing is fun!" said Antonio.

"Oh yeah?" Franco asked. "Try gutting a 40-pound salmon!"

The boys cleaned the deck. Rafael put the gear away. Andre drove the *Neptune*. They headed to a small cove. It was safe there. The water wasn't rough. They would stop. And they would sleep there. An hour later, they arrived. Then Andre tied up the boat.

"Tomorrow we will go deeper out to sea. That is where the halibut are," Andre said.

"I can't wait," Franco said. "But can we eat now? I'm hungry!"

Rafael laughed. "I was waiting for you to ask. You're always hungry!" said Rafael.

Everyone helped make dinner. It was salmon and rice and salad. Everyone was starving. They ate fast. The salmon was the best.

"Tomorrow is going to be different," Andre said.

"Aren't we fishing?" asked Antonio.

"Yes we are," said Andre. "But catching halibut is harder. The boat is anchored. We have to get our lines down far. Halibut live deep underwater."

"How far down?" Franco asked.

"About 150 feet," Andre said. "It's a lot of work to pull one in."

"We've all had a big day. We need rest," said Rafael.

Everyone was tired. They all went to bed.

Chapter 5

Morning came fast. Franco and Antonio got up. They ran to the deck. It wasn't sunny. Antonio looked sad.

"Don't worry," said Andre. "Fish like when it's cloudy. They bite more."

"Cool," Antonio said.

"Okay guys! Ready to catch some halibut?" Rafael asked.

They got to work fast. Andre got the gear. They needed special rods.

They also needed weights. Weights made the lines sink. They used five-pound weights.

Rafael drove the boat. He headed out to sea. They needed to go deep. Rafael drove for an hour. Then he stopped the boat.

"Perfect!" Andre yelled. "We are in 160 feet of water."

Rafael dropped anchor. He cut the engine. It was time to start fishing.

"Watch me first," said Andre.

Andre tied a weight to his rod. He dropped his line. It sank fast. The boys did the same.

"Move your rod," said Andre. "Move it back and forth."

He showed them how. Antonio and Franco did it too.

"Mine's stuck," Antonio said.

Andre and Rafael laughed. Antonio and Franco looked at them.

"Huh? What?" asked Antonio.

"It's not stuck," Rafael said. "It's a halibut!"

"Are you ready?" asked Andre.

Antonio was ready. He shook his head yes. He tried to pull it in. It wouldn't move. The fish was fighting. It was fighting hard. Antonio had to pull hard. He wasn't as strong as Franco, who was older. It was work!

Antonio was tired. After 20 minutes, he saw the fish. Andre grabbed a net. He scooped up the halibut. He dropped it on the deck. Everyone looked at it. Antonio's arms were tired. This halibut was big.

Fishing was good all morning. By noon, they caught six more halibut. Andre cleaned each one. This time Antonio helped gut the fish. But no one got a shooter. The biggest halibut was Antonio's first catch!

There wasn't room to store any more fish. The *Neptune* was full. They had to go to shore. The village of Hoonah was close. It had a fish-packing plant.

"They'll freeze our fish," said Andre. "Then they'll ship it to Juneau. We can pick it up there."

"Great," Franco said. "I thought we'd have to stop fishing!"

"No way," said Rafael. "We still have four more days!"

Rafael pulled the anchor. The *Neptune* headed to Hoonah.

Hoonah wasn't far. Packing the fish didn't take long. But everyone was tired. They spent the night in Hoonah.

Morning came fast again. The boys went for a run. They were happy to be on land. They loved the *Neptune*. But it was small. They needed the run. Breakfast was ready when they got back.

"What's up for today?" Franco asked.

"I asked Andre that too," said Rafael.

"Let's go back by that island. We had good luck there. I say we try again," Andre said.

"I'm in," Antonio said.

"You're the captain, Andre. Let's go," Rafael said.

They got ready fast. The *Neptune* headed out to sea again. Rafael drove first.

It was a nice day. The sun was out. The water was calm. Everyone enjoyed the ride.

Rafael saw something. He called for Andre. It was another boat. A man on the boat waved to them.

"What's going on Andre?" asked Rafael.

"It looks like he's waving at us. Maybe he needs help. Let's go see," Andre said.

Rafael drove to the other boat. He saw three men. They wore black clothes. They did not look friendly. Rafael didn't like them. He thought something was strange.

"Ahoy! Anything wrong?" Andre asked.

"Our boat broke. Can you tow us?" one of the men said.

"Sure thing," Andre said.

Rafael got closer. Franco threw them a rope. But they didn't catch it. The men jumped on the *Neptune*. They had guns! They pointed the guns at the Silvas and Andre.

The *Neptune* was hijacked!

Chapter 6

One man aimed his gun at them. The other two went back to their boat. They got six big boxes. They brought the boxes on the *Neptune*. The boxes looked heavy.

Andre was mad. He yelled at the men.

"What's going on? What are you doing?" Andre yelled.

But no one said anything.

"Let's get out of here!" one of the hijackers said.

"What's going on?" Andre yelled again.

A hijacker looked at Andre. "You ask too many questions," he said.

"Lock them in the back cabin. They won't get out," the other hijacker said.

Rafael was scared. He didn't want his sons to get hurt.

The hijackers pushed them in the cabin. They locked the door. They started the boat. The *Neptune* headed out to sea again. She wasn't on a fishing trip this time!

Franco and Antonio were scared.

"Who are these guys?" Franco asked.

"What's going on?" Antonio asked.

"I don't know who they are," said Andre. "And I don't know what's going on. But I know it's not good."

The cabin was small. And it was hot. There was no room to move.

Antonio sat on the floor. He looked at his dad. He was mad. He was happy fishing. Now he was a captive. It wasn't fair.

Then he heard a voice. It came from above. The control room was above them. He listened closely. It was the hijackers. He could hear them. Maybe he could find out what was going on.

"Dad," said Antonio. "I can hear them."

"Climb to the top bunk, Antonio. Listen to what they say," Rafael said.

Antonio climbed up. He put his

ear to the ceiling. He could hear every word they said.

"I can't believe our boat broke," one hijacker said.

"We got this boat," said a second hijacker. "We can still get to the pipeline. We'll get him the bombs in time."

"What do we do with them?" asked the third hijacker.

"We get rid of them," the second hijacker said.

"Wait a minute!" yelled the first hijacker. "We can't kill them! Blowing up the pipeline is one thing. But I'm not a killer!"

"I don't like it either. But we can't let them go. We have no choice," the second hijacker said.

Chapter 7

Antonio heard enough. He got off the top bunk. He looked at his dad.

"What did you hear?" Rafael asked.

"A lot," Antonio said. "And it's all bad. These guys are terrorists. They're going to blow up the pipeline. Then they're going to kill us!"

"Oh my God!" Andre cried. "This is serious."

"Yeah," said Rafael. "It's worse than I thought."

"You need a gun to catch shooters, right? Do you have one, Andre?" Antonio asked.

"I do. It's here in my bag," said Andre. "But one gun against terrorists? You heard them. They will shoot us."

"We need to surprise them," Rafael said. "They don't know we have a gun."

"But we're locked in!" Franco said. "How can we surprise them?"

"There's another way out," said Andre.

There was a secret door. It led to a locker. It was very small. The locker opened to the deck.

“Could we crawl through?” Franco asked.

“Maybe,” said Andre. “The door is small. Antonio may fit. The rest of us won’t.”

Rafael looked at Antonio. He looked worried.

“Dad,” Antonio said. “I know this is crazy. But it’s our only hope. Tell me what to do. I’ll do it. I can save us.”

Rafael had a plan. But he needed Antonio’s help. The plan was easy. They would surprise the terrorists. Rafael told Antonio the plan.

“Antonio, you need to get to the deck. You’ll crawl through the secret door. You’ll open the locker. You’ll be on deck. Then sneak back here.

Unlock the door. Then Andre and I will do the rest," said Rafael.

"Andre, you go to the front of the control room. I'll go to the back. Come through the front. Point the gun at them. I'll come through the back. They will be surprised. We'll trap them," Rafael said.

"Sounds good," said Andre. "Let's go get them!"

Chapter 8

Antonio crawled through the secret door. Then he opened the locker. The deck was empty! He was on the deck! It was dark. And he was scared. What if the terrorists saw him? But he couldn't think about that. He walked fast. He was quiet. Antonio knew he had to keep going. The terrorists were going to kill them. This was their only chance!

Antonio got to the cabin. The key wasn't in the lock! The plan was ruined. He didn't know what to do. Antonio looked around. There was a mug. Antonio looked inside. A key was inside! He hoped it was the right one. Antonio put the key in the lock. He turned it. He heard a click. The door swung open!

"Good job!" Rafael said. "You guys stay put."

Rafael looked at Andre.

"Show time! Ready?" Rafael asked.

"Let's roll!" said Andre.

Rafael and Andre left the cabin. Andre held the gun tightly.

Andre walked to the control room. He threw open the door.

"Hands up!" Andre yelled. "I'll shoot the first person who moves!"

Rafael came through the back. The terrorists were surprised! They didn't move. Andre pointed the gun at them. Rafael took their guns.

Soon the terrorists were tied up. Franco tied their hands and feet. Antonio tied them to the railing.

Chapter 9

Andre got on the radio. He called the coast guard. He told them what happened. Help was on the way.

"We did good today," Franco said. "We didn't catch any halibut. But we did catch three bigger fish!"

Alex Plummer was in the coast guard. He was a lieutenant. He went to help the *Neptune*. Lieutenant Plummer arrested the terrorists.

Then he took the boxes.

"You guys did great. You took down terrorists," Plummer said.

"My little bro did all the work," Franco said. "He unlocked the door. Good thing he did. We'd still be locked up. Or we'd be dead!"

Plummer smiled at Antonio.

"You're a hero," said Plummer. "Thank you."

"Um, sir? What was in those boxes?" asked Antonio.

"You guys were lucky. There were lots of explosives in those boxes," replied Plummer. "I still have work to do," he said. "We still need to know their plans. The FBI will ask them. Thanks again for your help. I am sorry this ruined your fishing."

“I think we’re going to head in. We’re tired after all the excitement. I think we need land,” Andre said. He looked tired.

“You should fish. You’ll catch a big one. Then you’ll forget about this mess. Fishing is the best way to relax!” said the lieutenant.

“I hope you’re right,” Rafael said.

The coast guard and terrorists headed to Juneau. Andre and Rafael took Lieutenant Plummer’s advice. They decided to fish.

They caught four more salmon. Fishing helped them forget the terrorists.

Everyone cleaned the fish. And they had fresh salmon for dinner. It was the best meal they ever ate.

They were all tired. No one slept the night before. The sun was low. But it hadn't set. All four fell asleep quickly.

Chapter 10

The terrorists were in jail. The FBI tried to get their plans. They wanted the terrorists to confess.

Special Agent Guzman worked for the FBI. Busting terrorists was his job.

"Let's find out who these guys work for," Guzman said. "They can tell us who's in charge. This bombing was stopped. But they will try again.

We have to get to their boss."

"They aren't talking," said another agent.

"We need to trick one. Make him think the other two blame him. It'll scare him. We'll make him talk," said Guzman.

They picked the youngest terrorist. He looked scared. They lied to him. The young man started to cry. He told the agents everything.

"I didn't want to do it!" the terrorist said. "They talked me into it!"

The terrorist told the truth. He told them the plan. He showed them their hideout. He named his boss. Guzman was happy. His trick worked. The pipeline was saved!

The Silvas fishing trip was over. They headed back to Juneau.

The *Neptune* pulled into the dock. Plummer and Guzman were there. So was the mayor of Juneau. They were smiling at Antonio.

"Thank you from the city of Juneau. We have something for you," the mayor said.

She gave Antonio an award. Everyone clapped.

It read:

To Antonio Silva

You are a hero.

The city of Juneau thanks you.

Rafael hugged Antonio. Franco gave him a fist bump.

"You saved our lives," Andre said.

"It wasn't that hard," said

Antonio. “I guess being smaller is good sometimes!”

“Our trips are never boring,” Franco said. “We caught a lot of fish. Almost got killed. And Antonio saved the pipeline. Mom will freak out.”

Rafael sighed. His sons were right. The Silva’s trips were never boring! Just once, he wanted to come home to the Heights without a scary story.